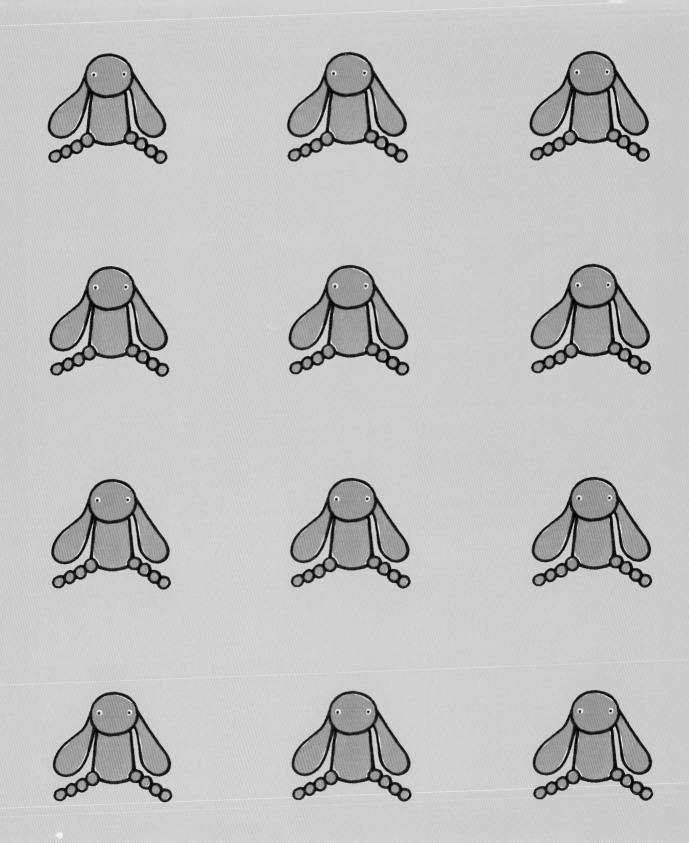

MYRIAD BOOKS LIMITED
35 Bishopsthorpe Road, London SE26 4PA

First published in Belgium and the Netherlands in 2006 by Clavis Uitgeverij,
Hasselt-Amsterdam.

Text and illustrations copyright © 2006 Clavis Uitgeverij, Hasselt-Amsterdam.
All rights reserved.
www.clavisbooks.com

Judith Koppens has asserted her right under the Copyright, Designs and Patents
Act 1998 to be identified as the author of this work.

All rights reserved. No part of this publication may be reproduced, stored
on a retrieval system, or transmitted in any form or by any means, electronic,
mechanical, photocopying, recording or otherwise, without the prior permission
of the copyright owners.

ISBN 1 84746 069 0
EAN 978 184746 069 1

Printed in China

Judith Koppens

Little Bear is ill

MYRIAD BOOKS LIMITED

"I don't feel like playing," says Little Bear.

"I feel a bit tired."

"I'm not hungry. I don't want to eat."

"I feel dizzy. And my tummy hurts."

"What is wrong with you?" Mummy Bear asks.
"You haven't eaten anything yet."

"Let me look at you," says Mummy Bear.
"Your head feels hot."

"You are ill. Let me take you to bed," Mummy Bear says.
"Bring your cuddly toy with you."

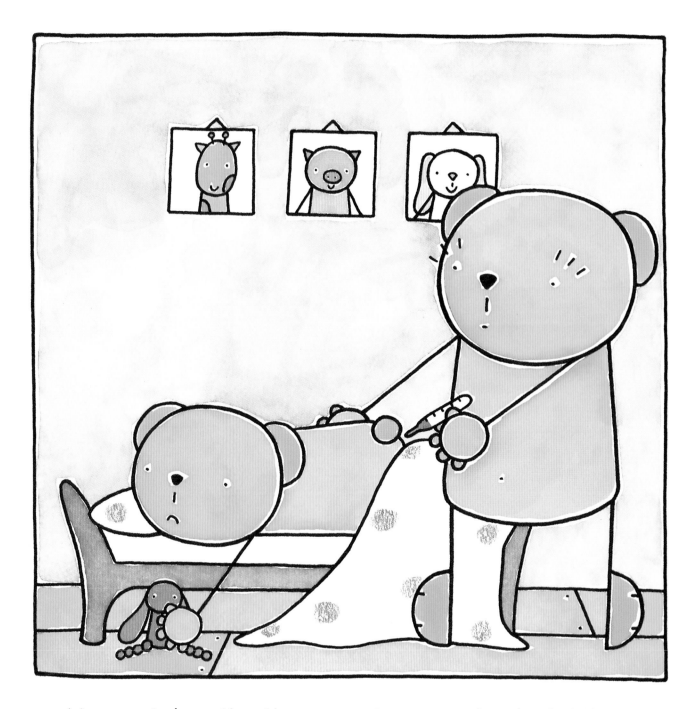

Mummy takes the thermometer and checks Little Bear's temperature.

"You have a fever, Little Bear," says Mummy Bear.

Mummy Bear gives Little Bear a pill
and a glass of water.

"Drink this and you will feel better", she says.
"Ooh, it doesn't taste nice," says Little Bear.

"I'll close the curtains and switch off the light,"
says Mummy Bear.

"Try to go to sleep now," says Mummy Bear.
"Oh dear! Being ill is no fun," says Little Bear.

When Little Bear wakes up, he feels a lot better.
"Mummy," he calls out, "can I come downstairs?"

"Your head doesn't feel so hot any more," says Mummy Bear. "Why don't you come and lie down on the couch with your cuddly toy?"

Mummy picks Little Bear's favourite book.
"I will read you a story," she says.

"Yippee!" says Little Bear. "I like having a story."

Mummy gives Little Bear a glass of apple juice with a straw. "Drink that, it's good for you," says Mummy Bear.

"Mmm!" says Little Bear. "I like apple juice."

"Look, Little Bear, you have a visitor," says Mummy.
"Hullo, Little Bear," says Pig.

"I have made you a drawing, because you are ill."
"Oh!" says Little Bear. "Thank you very much, Pig."

Pig and Little Bear sit on the sofa.
"Is it terrible to be ill?" Pig asks.

"Well..." smiles little Bear, "sometimes being ill is fun!"

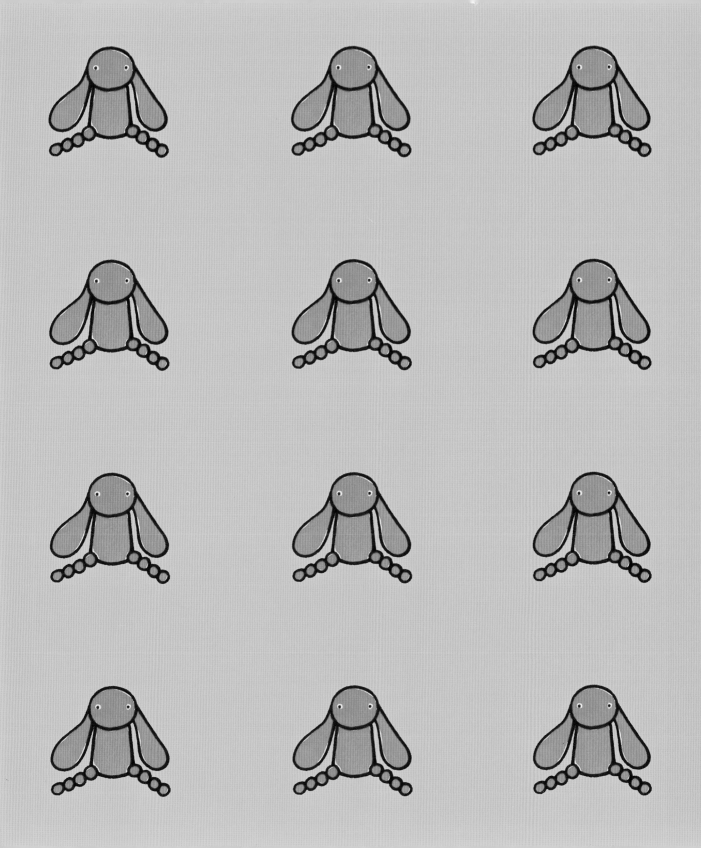